To the librarian who gave me the title of this book
and all the other librarians too —M.B.

For Kay —G.P.

Balzer + Bray is an imprint of HarperCollins Publishers.

I Love You Like a Pig
Text copyright © 2017 by Mac Barnett
Illustrations copyright © 2017 by Greg Pizzoli

ISBN 978-0-06-235483-9

The artist used Photoshop to create the digital illustrations for this book.
Typography by Greg Pizzoli
17 18 19 20 21  PC  10 9 8 7 6 5 4 3 2
❖
First Edition

I LOVE YOU
LIKE A PIG

Written by **Mac Barnett**

Illustrated by **Greg Pizzoli**

OINK
OINK

BALZER + BRAY
*An Imprint of HarperCollinsPublishers*

I love you
like a pig.

OINK        OINK

I'm happy
like a monster.

I'm lucky
like a window.

I'm smiling
like a tuna.

Because I love
you like a pig.

OINK                    OINK

You're funny
like a fossil.

You're sweet
like a banker.

You're crazy
like raspberries.

And I love you
like a pig.

I like you
like a tree.

I like you
like a rowboat.

I like you
like bread and milk.

But I love you
like a pig.

OINK OINK OINK